THIS
BOOK
BELONGS
TO

For our boy, Sam Lockie
A.S.

PUFFIN BOOKS

UK | USA | Canada | Ireland | Australia | India | New Zealand | South Africa

Puffin Books is part of the Penguin Random House group of companies whose
addresses can be found at global.penguinrandomhouse.com.

www.penguin.co.uk
www.puffin.co.uk
www.ladybird.co.uk

Penguin
Random House
UK

First published 2020

001

Printed in China

A CIP catalogue record for this book is available from the British Library

ISBN: 978–0–241–44190–9

All correspondence to:
Puffin Books, Penguin Random House Children's
One Embassy Gardens, 8 Viaduct Gardens, London SW11 7BW

MIX
Paper from
responsible sources
FSC® C018179
FSC
www.fsc.org

THE BEAR IN THE STARS

ALEXIS SNELL

PUFFIN

There once was a bear, a great white bear, Queen of Beasts.
Her kingdom was a beautiful, cold, glistening place.

The night skies above her realm were filled with shooting stars
and the shimmering Northern Lights.

But over the years the ice disappeared,
slipping away
like sand
through an hourglass.

And slowly, slowly, one by one, the other animals moved on.
The Great Bear had no food, and wherever she looked there was
only sea. Her snowy kingdom was melting away.

She had to leave.

The Great Bear crossed the crashing waves and raging seas.
She swam for what felt like forever, until finally she reached a glacier.
It was cold and icy, and she felt right at home.

But then the seasons changed.
The sun shone on the ice and the ice became a river.

The ice cracked,
    and the water trickled;
        downstream rushed the river,
           and downstream whooshed the bear.

On dry land, the trees were a vivid green and the flowers were
the most amazing colours, especially to a bear who had always lived in a
completely white world. The Great Bear felt a pang of hunger.
Where can I find food that's fit for a bear? she wondered.

On the edge of a forest she met a big black bear.
The bear was kind, and told her about a cool lake,
rich with many fish. The Great Bear thanked her new friend
and, driven forward by her hunger, she set out to find the lake.

When Bear reached the lake she bathed in it,

and ate a hundred fish.

Her belly was full again and she was happy.
But over time, the sun grew hotter and the fish were fewer.
Bear had to find food and somewhere cool.

She climbed hills, up and down,
finding fleeting shade in the shadows of the pines.

Her thick white fur, so useful in her icy kingdom,
was now too hot and too heavy. It felt suffocating.

She rested under some lemon trees and tried the fruit.
The lemons were juicy but so sour they made her nose tingle.
(Lemons are not bear food.)

The sun went down and the moon rose, and with it the stars shone brightly.
They were old friends to Bear, and they made her feel at home.

The world might have changed, she thought, but the stars are always here.

One morning, as the sun beat down, there was an unfamiliar noise in the canopy above. Bear raised her heavy head and saw a troop of monkeys chattering loudly.

The monkeys had never seen fur so white, or a bear so large. They saw at once that this was not the place for her.

"Come with us – we know a place that may help you,"
hollered the monkeys, and they swung from tree to tree
as Bear thudded beneath them.

They walked for hours and hours.

As day turned into night, the ground became hard under Bear's paws.
The air was thick with smoke, and the twinkling white stars
were obscured by dazzling lights of every colour.

They had reached a human town.

The monkeys led Bear to a building.
It was big and echoey and . . .
Oh so cool! thought Bear.

Bear stretched out on the cold, hard floor. She thanked the monkeys as they bounded away. Then she slept and slept and slept.

As daylight broke, Bear awoke to the sound of her
growling stomach, and a much louder noise . . .

The building had filled with
loud,
shouty,
busy,
bustling
humans!

She thought about eating a human;
there were so many of them.

When the humans saw her,
  some ran away yelling and screeching.
    Others drove her out of the cool building,
      chasing her with sticks, pushing her to the outskirts of town.

"Leave, Old Bear!" they shouted.
"We don't want you here – this is our kingdom!"

            Bear ran and ran until she could run no more.
            She slumped down, panting in the midday heat.

"Hello, Old Bear," came a tiny voice.

Bear opened her tired eyes to find herself face to face
with a very small human.

"Would you like an ice cream?"

Bear gulped down the sweet, icy treat,
which seemed to be made from snow and reminded her of home.

In the shade of a tree they sat together,
and Bear told the tiny human tales of her home
and stories of the stars.

But it wasn't long before the big humans returned
and chased Bear away.

As she left the tiny human, Bear wept.

Where can I go? I used to have a place in the world.
But now I have no kingdom, and I am the last of my kind.

As night fell, the shouting humans grew quiet,
and Bear searched for somewhere to rest.

At least it's cooler at night, she thought.

Bear gazed up into the night sky and felt a strange calmness.

Perhaps that's it, she thought. *I need to stay in the night always.*

The Great Bear, Queen of Beasts, gritted her teeth
and forced her tired body to run, faster and faster.

She jumped higher and higher as her white coat shone in the moonlight.

And, with one final leap,
she launched herself into the night sky.

Up, up and up . . .

Her white fur became twinkling dots in the cool,
quiet darkness of space.

The stars made a gentle music that echoed throughout the sky.
A kingdom she could rule over forever – Queen of the Stars.

While the sky
was icy cool,

the Earth below was growing hotter
and hotter.

The humans left behind knew that something had to change.
But was it too late?

A small human with a hopeful heart looked up at the sky.
Up above, Bear was sure she could see an old friend watching.

Perhaps if I helped them, thought the Bear, *the creatures of Earth would begin to look after their world?*

Perhaps . . .

The Great Bear thought about the hardships she had faced,
but she also remembered the kindnesses.

She whispered to the stars around her . . .

. . . and slowly, slowly, the stars began sending sparks
of cool blue light tumbling through the darkness:

first one by one,

then two by two,

then more:

hundreds,

thousands,

millions.

Stardust! It fell through the night sky
and landed on Earth in huge, white, icy drifts.

The icy drifts melted gently. Small shoots appeared,
bees went to work, and the earth hummed with new life.
Humans and animals looked after the world together.

The Queen of the Stars smiled down
at the newly peaceful world.

And the little one looked up and whispered . . .

"Thank you, Great Bear."

Goodnight, little one.

I wrote this story when my son was not yet two. I want him to know the wonder and awe that can come from the natural world, but also the realities and hardships that we are now facing. In my story I use a little bit of magic to make things right, but it's not too late for us to use our natural ingenuity and creativity to make the changes we need to help our world recover from the damage we have caused. Kindness and respect for our environment, and for others who are a little different from ourselves, is so important. Also important to my son are bears and stars and moons and, of course, ice cream.

– Alexis Snell